It was the night before the Fourth of July, 1976...

Deep in the Roxbury night, the peace and quiet was suddenly torn asunder by a thundering *boom*. It was so loud, it sounded like it was coming from right outside Amy's window.

Instantly, she sprang awake and shot out of bed, half falling onto the floor. The 15-year-old pulled herself up and shook her head hard, trying to clear away the cobwebs clogging her mind.

Before she could get to her bedroom window to see what was happening, another boom rang out, followed by a series of short, chattering bursts. She dropped back onto her bed, stunned by the sudden cacophony, unable to think straight long enough to figure out what had caused it.

Then, without warning, something crashed through her window and flew across the room, shedding sparks along the way.

As Amy cried out, the object crashed into the wall and exploded. Fiery pieces of debris showered her dresser and carpet, even landing on her bed.

Bottle rocket. That, she realized, was what had smashed through her window. And all the noise that had preceded it could only have come from one source—a source she knew was plentiful in the Lindsey family's back yard shed.

Fireworks.

Colorful lights flared through the broken window, playing over the spots of flame that were igniting all over the room from the bottle rocket.

Eyes wide, Amy leaped off the bed and ran out of her room while she still could. As she hurled open her door, she saw Mom running toward her, wrapped in a bathrobe.

"Let's go!" Mom grabbed her hand and pulled her into the hall. "Come on, hurry!"

Fourth of July at Glosser's

Glosser Bros. Holidays
Book 7

By Robert Jeschonek

pie press publishing

FIRST PIE PRESS EDITION, JULY 2020

Copyright © 2020 Robert Jeschonek
www.robertjeschonek.com

Cover Art Copyright © 2020 Ben Baldwin
www.benbaldwin.co.uk

All rights reserved.

This book is a work of fiction. Names, characters, places and incidents either are products of the author's imagination or are used fictitiously. Any resemblance to actual events or locales or persons, living or dead, is entirely coincidental.

Published in July 2020 by arrangement with the author. All rights reserved by the author.

A Pie Press book

pie press publishing
www.piepresspublishing.com

For information about permission to reproduce sections from this book, write to piepress@piepresspublishing.com.

The text was set in Myriad Pro and Garamond.
Book design by Robert Jeschonek

ISBN-13: 9780998576183

DEDICATION

To 1976, the end of an era in Johnstown.
We will never see its like again.

"Can we light one *now*, Grandpa? *Can* we?"

Amy Lindsey's little redheaded brother ran out of the house first, leaving her and Mom in the dust. The kid was so worked up, Amy thought he might explode.

The heap of fireworks in the trunk of her grandpa's old Chevy was a dream come true for the seven-year-old, whose nickname, after all, was...

"Boom, no," said Grandpa. "You *know* these are for the Fourth of July."

"Just one!" Boom's hand snapped out, reaching for a bottle rocket. His actual name was Boone, but Boom fit him for obvious reasons. "Just a test fire!"

It was then that Mom intervened, grabbing his wrist. "I *think* you can wait *two nights*. We have to keep up the tradition, don't we, Amy?"

All eyes were on Amy, as if the 15-year-old with the short auburn hair had any great interest in the tradition... especially these days. Why bother trying to keep a family tradition going when the family itself was falling apart?

But Amy played along. "That's right." She nodded for Boom's benefit.

"And this has to be the biggest year yet," added Grandpa. "It'll be the Bicentennial, remember," he said, as if anyone could possibly forget. As if anyone in Johnstown, Pennsylvania could talk about anything else with July 4th, 1976 just two days away.

Especially now that Paul Newman the movie star had left town.

With one hand restrained by Mom, Boom grabbed with the other for a sphere wrapped in brown paper, but she jerked him back, and he missed it.

"Nooo!" squawked Boom. "I just wanna light *one!* Just *one!*"

"Just wait till Monday," Mom said firmly, pulling him away from the bed of the truck. "We'll have our very own Bicentennial spectacle."

Grandpa smiled. "You better believe it. I must've bought all the fireworks in the state of West Virginia!"

"More than Dad?" asked Boom.

At that, everyone got quiet all of a sudden. Dad was the one who had made the traditional fireworks run every year, driving south of the Pennsylvania border where buying fireworks wasn't breaking the law (though bringing them back over the border was). Dad was the one who had hauled the fireworks, set them up, and set them off on the Fourth, providing a free show that he claimed was better than the one sponsored by the Glosser Bros. Department Store. Dad was the one who'd done all that.

And now Dad wasn't around. He was no longer part of the family. He didn't live in the little white house on the wooded double lot on top of a hill in Roxbury with them anymore.

"You be the judge, Boom." Grandpa chuckled and tousled Boom's wild red hair. "I did the best I could, buying all this stuff and driving it here. You tell me Monday night if I did as well as your dad."

"I will! Don't worry!" Boom's eyes were drawn back to the heap of fireworks. His fingers twitched as if he were ready to snatch up handfuls and run.

"In the meantime, I better get these unloaded." Grandpa scooped up a bunch of rockets and headed for the shed in the back yard, giving Mom a look on the way past. "I just hope none are missing by the time I get back."

Mom nodded. "Boom, honey, I need you and Amy to come with me and pick up some decorations and picnic stuff. Let's go."

Boom's shoulders slumped. "Aw, Mom." He stared at the fireworks in the trunk a long time...but then he turned and followed Mom.

As for Amy, she fell in step, too. "Where are we going?"

"Glosser's." Mom smiled at her. "Where else?"

*****

The Glosser Bros. Department Store in downtown Johnstown could not have been more patriotic. Everywhere Amy looked as she walked through the ground floor, there were red, white, and blue streamers, American flags, and images of fireworks, the Declaration of Independence, President George Washington, and the

Liberty Bell. Mannequins were dressed in Colonial outfits, some armed with muskets and wearing tri-corner hats. The "Star-Spangled Banner" played over the P.A. system speakers, along with John Philip Sousa marches and other patriotic music.

Signs amid the racks and tables of merchandise announced the big fireworks show at Point Stadium on July Fourth, sponsored by Glosser Bros.—but seeing them made Amy feel sad. She couldn't help remembering what her dad had always said when he'd seen those signs and how it had made her laugh.

They need to update that sign. Change it to "The Don't-Bother Fourth of July So-Called Fireworks," as in "Nowhere near as good as the spectacular in the Lindsey family's backyard in Roxbury, so don't bother coming."

She'd loved hearing him say that, even if he'd had alcohol on his breath at the time. The alcohol had rarely bothered her, actually, except once in a while, when he'd had too much. Even then, it hadn't always been a problem—except when "silly Dad" turned into "angry Dad" and argued with Mom.

Would Amy ever hear him say those words again? She didn't think so. Dad wasn't coming back, according to Mom—and neither was Amy's older brother, Mark... fun-loving, loveable Mark. She'd always adored and looked up to him, and he'd always been there for her—until the 19-year-old had walked out the door after Dad, that is. Mark had gone to look after him, he'd insisted, because Dad didn't seem to be in his right mind...but the end result was the same whatever the reason. Dad and Mark were both gone.

And it was all because of that stupid Paul Newman.

"Hey, these are fun." Mom picked up boxes of sparklers from one of the tables. "Maybe I'll buy a few."

Boom sighed loudly and shook his head. "Waste of money, Mom. We won't need those with all the firepower we'll be setting off."

"Okay then." Mom put the sparklers down and moved to another table that was heaped with decorations. "I'll use my employee discount for something else."

Amy trailed after them, her hands idly drifting over items on the tables and in the bins. Mom worked at Glosser's, and Amy loved to go there—but the place wasn't lifting her spirits today.

As mean as Dad had been in moving away, it just didn't feel like the Fourth of July without him.

"These are perfect." Mom gathered up rolls of red, white, and blue crepe paper and dropped them in the wire basket she carried. She threw in some cardboard cutouts, too—images of American flags, hot dogs, hamburgers, apple pie, and fireworks. "We'll have a real Bicentennial blast, you guys."

Suddenly, Amy couldn't take it anymore. When Mom's back was turned, she darted away down the aisle and ducked into an open elevator as a young woman stepped out.

She hit the button for the second floor, and the door slid closed. When it opened again, she ran past racks of lingerie, dresses, and men's suits, and sprinted through the tunnel to the Cafeteria building next door, heading for her favorite place in her favorite department store.

*****

"Hello, Amy." Ruby Shaffer smiled and waved from behind the counter of the Glosser Bros. soda fountain. "So nice to see you, dear."

For the first time that day, Amy managed a genuine smile. Ruby—and her twin sister, Ruth, who also worked the soda fountain—had known Amy for as long as she could remember. They had a way of making her feel better no matter what...and the free samples of ice cream they gave her were just one small part of it.

"Hi, Ruby." Amy managed half a smile as she folded her arms on the counter.

"All ready for the Fourth?" asked Ruby.

Amy shook her head. "How about you?"

"Just the usual." The little brown-haired woman in the red Glosser Bros. smock shrugged. "Going to Point Stadium for Glosser's fireworks with Ruth." She hiked a thumb over her shoulder toward the kitchen door. "Plus watching the Bicentennial celebrations on TV, of course."

"I just wish it was over," said Amy.

Ruby frowned. "Now why do you say that?"

Amy shrugged. "Reminds me too much of how things used to be, I guess."

Ruby reached out and patted her arm. "With your dad, you mean. And your brother."

Amy nodded. "I hate how things are now. I just hate 'em."

"But you still have your mother and little brother," said Ruby. "And your grandpa. And me and Ruth."

"I wish Paul Newman had never come here." Amy felt

tears welling in her eyes. "I wish he'd just stayed in stupid Hollywood."

Ruby frowned. She was just about to ask a question when Amy's mom rushed out of the tunnel from Glosser's second floor with Boom in tow.

"There you are!" Mom looked suddenly relieved. "I *thought* this was where I'd find you."

Amy wiped the tears from her eyes and turned to face her. "Uh-huh."

"Thanks, Ruby," said Mom.

"Any time, sweetie." Ruby still looked concerned. "No trouble at all."

Mom took a good look at Amy and seemed to catch on. "You know what? Could you fix us a couple hot fudge sundaes, Rube?"

"Well, sure." Ruby smiled. "One for each of the kids?"

Mom nodded, then shook her head. "You know what? Make it three. I think we could all use a treat today."

"And what else?" asked Ruby.

"Extra sprinkles!" shouted Boom.

"Will do." Ruby winked at Amy. "And extra fudge for you."

Amy nodded. She wouldn't turn it down.

*****

When Mom, Boom, and Amy got home, her best friend Kim Evans was sitting on the front steps, waiting for them.

"Hey!" Kim lived a street away. She and Amy had

been friends since second grade. "What took you so long?" She grinned and got to her feet.

Amy plodded from the car to the steps, unable to summon much enthusiasm. Even a surprise visit from her best friend felt like an annoyance today.

"We were just picking up some decorations for our big Bicentennial party." Mom hefted her white Glosser Bros. shopping bag with the brown stripes down the side. "You're coming, aren't you, Kim?"

Kim patted her tightly braided corn rows. "Well, I'd *like* to." She winced. "That's kind of why I'm here, Mrs. Lindsey."

"Oh?" Mom tipped her head to one side, looking concerned.

"See, my family is going out of town." Kim folded her skinny brown arms over her pink t-shirt. "Tomorrow. I can't make it to the party."

"That's too bad, honey," said Mom.

"Where're you going?" asked Amy.

"Actually," said Kim, "the question is, where are *we* going?" A huge, bright smile spread over her face as her dark eyes fixed on Amy.

"Huh?" Amy frowned.

Kim grabbed her hands and shook them giddily. "*We* are going to *Washington, D.C.* for the big Bicentennial *fireworks* extravaganza!"

"We are?"

Kim looked in Mom's direction. "If it's *okay,* that is."

"Who's driving?" Mom seemed a little dazed.

"My dad," said Kim. "My mom and sisters are going, too, and we're staying with my cousins who live right in the city."

"Hmm." If Mom was thrilled with the idea, she didn't show it.

Amy, on the other hand, needed no persuading. Getting out of town would be the perfect way to put some distance between her and the bad feelings stirred up by the Fourth of July in Johnstown.

"Sounds great!" Amy squeezed Kim's hands back and beamed with delight. "Mom, can I go? Please?"

"What about the fireworks?" Mom nodded in the general direction of the shed where Grandpa had stowed his smuggled cargo. "Your grandfather says it'll be the best show yet."

"I know, but this is the *Bicentennial*," said Amy. "In the nation's *capital*."

"*Our* fireworks will be *better*," said Boom.

Amy let go of Kim's hands. "*Please*, Mom?" She folded her hands as if in prayer. "I don't want to *miss* this!"

Mom stared at Amy for a long moment, then sighed. "Okay." She still didn't sound thrilled. "As long as you let me know you're all right."

Amy unfolded her hands, wrapped them into fists, and shook them excitedly. "You know I will! Thanks, Mom!"

It was then that Boom stormed over and angrily jabbed a finger at both of them. "You're ruining everything! The biggest night of the year, and you're ruining it!"

With that, he whirled and ran off into the house, slamming the front door behind him.

But none of that bothered Amy in the slightest. All that mattered was being away from home on what was becoming her least favorite night of the year.

Which had been her dad's *most* favorite night until Paul Newman had come along and talked him into leaving them all behind and taking her brother Mark with him.

*****

Amy couldn't sleep that night, which made no sense. After all, she was getting out of being home for the Lindsey Family Fireworks Spectacular. She was going to Washington, D.C., where her family's breakup was bound to be the furthest thing from her mind.

She should have been relieved and sleeping soundly—so why was she wide awake at three in the morning? And why, every time she closed her eyes, did she see that actor on the ice of the local hockey rink, taking off his uniform a piece at a time while striptease music played from the loudspeakers?

Maybe because it had been the last time that she and her parents and brothers had been together, having fun?

It felt like she was being haunted by that moment, which was a scene from a movie. She and her family had been extras that day, along with several thousand other Johnstown residents—all cheering at the top of their lungs as the actor skated and stripped in the War Memorial Arena and the movie cameras rolled. It had seemed like so much fun at the time; how could she have known it would be the last fun her family would have together?

How could she have known that months later, she'd be haunted by the movie they were making? How could she have known that she'd be haunted by *Slap Shot?*

Pushing off the covers, Amy got out of bed and

padded out of her room. The house was dark and quiet, with everyone sound asleep. That in itself was unsettling, not at all the way things had been before. With Dad and Mark in the house, there had always been snoring and tossing and turning. Neither of them had been passive or quiet sleepers, which used to drive Amy crazy, always waking her up.

But now, there was just quiet. Except for the stripper music she heard when she closed her eyes.

The film crew was long gone now, and so was the cast. They'd come to make a movie about small-town hockey, based on the true story of the local Johnstown Jets, who'd won the championship in '75. For a few short months, they had turned the town into a mini-Hollywood, using local landmarks as sets and backdrops, using local people in bit parts and as extras...giving them a taste of the movie business magic. Letting them rub elbows with stars like the great Paul Newman.

Then they'd moved on in June, leaving hopes and dreams in their wake—and in some cases, wreckage.

Mom had gotten plenty of both. After the filming, her husband had left her—but during it, she'd been luckier than most.

Entering the living room, Amy saw the proof of that luck propped on an end table by the couch. A black-and-white 8 by 10 photo occupied a wooden frame, an image that captured the excitement of what had promised to be the biggest and best break of Mom's life.

In the photo, Mom and three other women were all laughing and holding up hockey sticks. They surrounded two men in hockey uniforms with "Chiefs" printed in bold letters across the chest—Michael Ontkean (who'd done the stripping) and the biggest star of the movie, one of the biggest stars in the world, whose bright eyes twinkled as he grinned self-effacingly.

There he was, the one and only Paul Newman.

Amy turned on the lamp on the table, picked up the photo, and stared. She remembered how thrilled Mom had been to get a small speaking role in the movie, playing the wife of one of the hockey players. Her community theater experience had really paid off, helping her audition well enough to get the part.

It had been a dream come true. Every day, she'd had more great stories to tell when she got home. Several times, she'd even brought Amy or Mark or Boom to the set during filming.

And when Paul had told her how well she was doing, it had made her feel like a million bucks. And when he'd written an encouraging message on the 8x10 photo, it had sent her straight into the stratosphere.

You're the real deal, Kelly. That was what he'd written in black Sharpie marker across the lower right corner. *Don't let anyone tell you otherwise.*

See you in Hollywood, Paul Newman.

Who would have thought such a wonderful message—such a wonderful experience—could lead to so much pain?

Sometimes, Amy just wanted to throw that photo in the garbage and forget about what had happened. Tonight, she settled for putting it face down on the end table, then dropping herself face down on the sofa. She just wanted to put *Slap Shot* and what had happened to her family right out of her mind.

Instead, as soon as she started to doze, the striptease music rose unbidden within her. Again, she saw Michael Ontkean skating around the rink, taking off one article of clothing after another.

Her eyes popped open. She had only been an extra in one scene, had never seen the finished film (which wouldn't premiere until the following year), and yet she couldn't get it out of her mind. It wouldn't stop haunting her.

She could only hope the Bicentennial fireworks in Washington, D.C. might finally drive it away...at least for a while. Paul Newman had done enough damage already.

She didn't want anything to do with him or his stupid movie, no matter what he'd written on Mom's picture.

No matter what he'd told Amy herself on his last day in town.

*****

After a night of very little sleep, Amy was dead on her feet the next day. If she hadn't already promised to help Mom on the job that morning, she never would have volunteered to go along and lend a hand.

"Thanks again, honey." Mom smiled as she drove the family car—a red '74 Ford Pinto—from Roxbury into town. "I really appreciate this."

"No problem." Amy blinked hard, clearing the sleepy haze from her eyes. She couldn't believe she was up and on the road at seven a.m. after sleeping maybe three hours thanks to visions of *Slap Shot*. All she wanted to do was roll over and drift off for the rest of the day.

"Well, the bosses will be glad to see you," said Mom.

"It means a lot that my daughter is helping set up Point Stadium for the big show."

"Good." Amy yawned as the Pinto rolled down Franklin Street past Conemaugh Hospital and next-door Mercy Hospital. Lots of people were already crisscrossing the street, some in blue-green surgical scrubs, some in white lab coats.

"These fireworks are the Glosser company's chance to shine, especially this year," said Mom. "Everybody's in the patriotic spirit because of the Bicentennial."

Not everybody, thought Amy. "Just so there's no hockey tribute," she mumbled.

"What was that?" asked Mom. "I didn't hear you."

"Nothing." Amy yawned again. "Just thinking out loud."

*****

"Kelly Lindsey! Thanks for coming!" Bill Glosser stood inside the gate of the stadium in his tweed suit and wire-framed glasses, grinning around the stem of his ever-present pipe. "And thank you for bringing along this lovely young assistant!"

Amy barely managed the slightest smile. She liked Bill, he was always wry and kind, but her lack of sleep continued to drag her down.

"As you can see, we have our work cut out for us." Bill turned and spread his arms to take in the stadium. Nothing had been done to decorate it, from what Amy could see. "And yet, I am confident we can make the magic happen in time. Do you know why?"

"Teamwork?" said Mom.

Bill chuckled, puffing pipe smoke over his shoulder. "The Bicentennial spirit!" he said. "I think we can all agree that it moves mountains."

Mom smiled at Amy. She, too, got a kick out of Bill. "Absolutely, we can all agree on that."

Amy just nodded and yawned.

"Let's get to it, shall we?" Bill navigated the cement walkway from the gate to the concession stand, and they followed. "Uncle Sam is depending on us."

The concession stand counter and the pavement in front of it were piled with cartons of decorations. Three twentysomething women in shorts and t-shirts were sorting through the contents, taking stock of what they had, and smiled when they saw Bill, Kelly, and Amy approach.

"Ladies," said Bill. "I bring you reinforcements."

The women all smiled and waved at Kelly and Amy, and they waved back.

"As for the plan, it is this," Bill said between smoky puffs. "Let your love of America guide your every move, in the name of Glosser Bros. and the hope that I will not hold up your efforts to relentless ridicule."

The women laughed and kept working. Kelly walked over to join them, and Amy started to follow.

But Bill caught her arm on the way past. "Not you, slugger." He pulled her along to a huge roll of white vinyl leaning against the wall of the concession stand. "There's a critical task with your name on it right here."

Pipe clamped firmly between his teeth, Bill picked up one end of the roll, and Amy got the other. Carrying the load between them, they crossed the field—set up as a baseball diamond for the summer—and climbed the steps up into the stands on the side opposite where they'd entered the park in the first place.

"Are you excited about the big show tomorrow night?" The higher they climbed, the more out of breath Bill sounded.

"Well..."

"What if I told you the fun quotient would be through the *roof* for *you* in particular?" Five rows from the top, Bill paused to rest. "What if I said *you* would have the honor of a *lifetime*?"

Amy cleared her throat, not sure where this was going. "I'd say I can't be here because..."

He turned and smiled, looking as amused and fatherly as ever. "You will be our button-pusher. The starter of the show. Like Lady Liberty, you will light the flames of freedom in the skies overhead."

She frowned. "But I..."

"It's a very great honor, you know," said Bill. "*Especially* on such an historic occasion. No one else will ever be able to say they pushed the button that set off the fireworks in Johnstown for the nation's Bicentennial."

This time, Amy said it loud and clear. "No." She shook her head emphatically. "Thank you for the honor, but I can't accept it. I won't be here."

"You won't?" Smoke obscured Bill's face as he puffed harder on the pipe.

"I'm going to Washington, D.C. with my best friend's family," explained Amy. "To see the Bicentennial fireworks."

"I can't argue, that's a wonderful opportunity." Bill

FOURTH OF JULY AT GLOSSER'S

nodded. "But so is this. Are you sure I can't talk you into staying?"

"Thank you, Mr. Glosser, but no."

"It's Bill," he told her. "And if you change your mind, the offer still stands." Smiling, he hefted his end of the roll and climbed the rest of the steps with Amy close behind.

When they got to the top of the stands, they unrolled the vinyl to reveal a giant red, white, and blue banner. Then they hung it from the rails along the back side of Point Stadium, unfurling it over the curved brick wall so drivers on the elevated Johnstown expressway could see it clearly as they passed.

Happy Bicentennial from Glosser Bros.! That was what it said, with the instantly recognizable Glosser Bros. logo in flowing script lettering and the star-shaped Bicentennial logo on either end.

"Not bad," said Bill as he and Amy leaned over the railing to admire their work. "We know how to put on a show here in Johnstown, too, don't we?"

"Uh-huh," said Amy, though she still wanted nothing more than to get out of town on the Fourth of July.

*****

Hours later, Mom and Amy wrapped up their work and left Point Stadium, heading for home. Mom wasn't done for the day; she still had to put in some hours at the store that afternoon. But Amy had worked hard at the Point, and Kim had mentioned getting together later to prep for D.C., so Mom wasn't going to drag things out.

Lunchtime traffic was heavy that day, so the ride up

Main Street was slow. Workers and shoppers hurried back and forth across the street, darting into restaurants like Johnnie's or stores like the Hello Shop or McCrory's.

Central Park was crowded, too, with people strolling along the sidewalks or sitting on benches among the trees and monuments to enjoy the midday sun and warmth.

Seeing all that, Amy remembered a scene from months ago, right there on that same street along that same park. Crowds had jammed every inch of the place, cheering and clapping as a parade passed between them—a fake victory parade staged by the film crew for the movie.

Actors playing hockey team members rode in convertibles up the street, waving and grinning as the crowd cheered their fictional victory. Paul Newman himself rode with Michael Ontkean and Lindsay Crouse (who played Michael's wife), flashing thumbs-ups as they slowly rolled past in a white Lincoln Continental draped with victory banners.

The scene was so vivid in Amy's mind, it was almost as if she'd traveled back in time to be a part of it all again. It was almost as if she were standing on the curb in front of the Embassy Theater, clapping as Mom rode by in one of the cars.

Closing her eyes, she fell instantly asleep and was lost in a dream of that moment...only this time, she was in the Continental with Paul Newman and Michael Ontkean instead of Lindsay Crouse. This time, she was waving at the crowd, drinking in the excitement.

And then Paul leaned over and whispered in her ear. The words were soft but plain as day, and she knew them very well.

They were the last words he'd said to her. As much as she hated him now, she always tried not to think about them...but there they were.

"Earth to Amy! Come in, Amy!"

Startled, Amy snapped her eyes open and was out of the dream. Mom, who'd said the words that had awakened her, gave her shoulder one last shake for good measure.

"Maybe you should take a nap when you get home, honey," said Mom. "You need to rest up if you're going to D.C. tomorrow."

Amy yawned, the memory of the parade echoing in her mind as Mom turned off Main Street. "I'm fine," she said. "Trust me, there's *no way* I'll sleep through those fireworks."

*****

"Knock knock. Anyone home?"

An hour and a half later, Amy was awakened by another voice—that of her best friend. Blinking her eyes open, she saw Kim's face through the darkened lenses of her sunglasses, smiling down at her.

It was then she quickly remembered where she was and how she'd gotten there.

"You just missed the handsomest boy," said Kim. "I nudged you, but I couldn't get you to wake up."

Propping herself up on her elbows, Amy looked around. From her perch on a chaise lounge in the sun, she scanned the deck of the bright blue swimming pool, taking in the swimmers and sunbathers crowding the cement and water alike.

"Don't worry." Kim chuckled. "There are always

plenty of good-looking guys at Bethco Pines."

"I can't argue with that," said Amy.

This, then, was their idea of packing and getting ready for the trip to D.C. Kim, who was old enough to drive, had borrowed her mom's car, picked up Amy, and driven to Bethco Pines in Somerset County.

It was their favorite place to hang out in the summer—a private club on the shore of the Quemahoning Reservoir, a half-hour drive from home. As the daughter of a boss at Bethlehem Steel in Johnstown, Kim was a member, and she borrowed her sister's pass to get Amy in free of charge without having to buy a guest pass.

What better way to spend a hot summer afternoon instead of staying home and packing suitcases indoors?

"You know we're going to see loads of cute guys in D.C., right?" Kim raised a half-empty bottle of Coke and had a sip.

"I thought we were going for the fireworks," said Amy.

"Oh, we'll see stars if they're cute enough." Kim laughed. "I can't *wait* to get there."

"Me, too."

Just then, the lifeguard blew his whistle and announced an adult swim. All the kids clambered out of the pool, whining every step of the way.

"This trip is going to be the best," said Kim. "I'm telling you, my cousins are *fun*."

"Thanks for rescuing me," said Amy. "Being stuck at home with my dad gone is like the saddest possible way to spend the Fourth of July."

"That's me." Kim smiled. "Coming to the rescue is what I do."

FOURTH OF JULY AT GLOSSER'S

Amy watched as the adult swim ran its course—a flock of mostly middle-aged women sedately paddling back and forth in the crystal blue waters. Meanwhile, the exiled kids lined the edge of the pool, staring furtively as they waited for the whistle to blow again, giving them the signal to dive-bomb back into the water as obnoxiously as possible.

"How's your dad doing, anyway?" asked Kim. "And your brother?"

"Beats me. I haven't talked to either of them since they left."

"By choice?"

Amy shrugged. "Maybe they don't have telephones where they went. Who knows?"

Kim sipped more Coke and put the bottle back down on the cement. "How long has it been, now? A month?"

"A little less, but it seems like a lot longer." Amy sighed. "I just wish things could go back to the way they were."

Kim swung her legs off the chaise and turned to face her. "What if he asked you to go live with him? Your dad, I mean. Would you go?"

Amy shook her head. "Not a chance, after what he did."

"What about Mark?"

"He just went along to watch out for Dad," said Amy. "It wasn't his idea."

"But you won't forgive your dad."

"Right," said Amy. "That'll never change."

"But what if it does? Maybe things won't seem so bad after a while."

"What if it was *your* dad?" asked Amy. "What if he

just up and left one day? Could you forgive him?"

Kim frowned, thinking it over. She opened her mouth to answer—but before she got the words out, the lifeguard blew the whistle.

All at once, every kid in the pool area hurled themselves into the water, raising an unholy splash that drenched the adults before they could escape.

Amy and Kim both watched, smirking, and shook their heads. Not long ago, they had been among that wild number, causing mischief with the glorious waters of Quemahoning Reservoir rippling in the background. Now, at ages 15 and 16, it all looked different. Their concerns and obsessions had changed.

Though, sometimes, Amy secretly wished they had never changed at all.

"Damn kids," she said as a joke.

"Seriously," said Kim. "Somebody oughtta go dunk their asses."

"Sounds like a plan." Amy settled back on the chaise and closed her eyes. "Just as soon as I map out our moves on the backs of my eyelids."

"No, wait." Kim shook her by the shoulder. "You have *got* to see the new lifeguard!"

Amy opened her eyes, again denied the rest she craved, and she didn't get another wink of sleep the whole time they were there at Bethco.

*****

That night, finally, Amy was able to sleep soundly. She went to bed early, not long after dinner, and fell instantly into the deepest of slumbers.

No dreams of *Slap Shot* disturbed her—no striptease music or visions of riding with Paul Newman in a Lincoln Continental in a victory parade. For once, her worried mind went blank, allowing her to completely relax and get the rest she needed for her busy day tomorrow in D.C.

But it didn't last.

Deep in the night, the peace and quiet was suddenly torn asunder by a thundering *boom*. It was so loud, it sounded like it was coming from right outside her window.

Instantly, Amy sprang awake and shot out of bed, half falling onto the floor. She pulled herself up and shook her head hard, trying to clear away the cobwebs clogging her mind.

Before she could get to her bedroom window to see what was happening, another boom rang out, followed by a series of short, chattering bursts. She dropped back onto her bed, stunned by the sudden cacophony, unable to think straight long enough to figure out what had caused it.

Then, without warning, something crashed through her window and flew across the room, shedding sparks along the way.

As Amy cried out, the object crashed into the wall and exploded. Fiery pieces of debris showered her dresser and carpet, even landing on her bed.

Bottle rocket. That, she realized, was what had smashed through her window. And all the noise that had preceded it could only have come from one source—a source she knew was plentiful in the Lindsey family's back yard shed.

Fireworks.

Again, there were percussive booms and chattering

cracks...then shrieking whistles and whooshing hisses one after another. Colorful lights flared through the broken window, playing on the walls, rug, and furniture, spraying over the spots of flame that were igniting all over the room from the bottle rocket.

The loudest blast yet went off next, shaking the floor under her feet. Another fiery missile flashed in through the window and blew against the wall, spreading more flames.

Eyes wide with fear, Amy leaped off the bed and ran out of her room while she still could. As she hurled open her door, she saw Mom running toward her, barefoot and wrapped in a red flannel bathrobe.

"Let's go!" Mom grabbed her hand and pulled her into the hall. "Come on, hurry!"

As they raced past open doorways, colored lights blazed across their path from within, cast from windows facing the back yard. The cascade of blasts continued, rattling glass and wood alike, roaring again and again in a terrible, deafening symphony.

Amy looked in every doorway they passed but saw no sign of her brother. "Where's Boom?" she shouted.

"I don't know!" yelled Mom. "He must be outside somewhere!"

As they sprinted toward the kitchen, something big smashed through a window and plowed through the hallway ahead of them. Mom flung herself back from the ball of flame, taking Amy down with her.

They heard the fireball collide with the living room wall and explode. Red and blue sparks showered in its wake, pulsing into the hall and kitchen like a fountain of hot, bright shrapnel.

"This way." Mom leaped to her feet and dragged Amy up with her. Without hesitation, she charged the rest of the way through the hall and hurtled across the kitchen.

Something whistled past behind them, but they made it through without being hit. Mom swung open the back door and barreled out onto the porch with Amy close behind.

They paused then and took in the scene...just long enough to see fireworks launching everywhere from the direction of the old wooden shed. The light show kept blasting away, seemingly inexhaustible, illuminating the yard in rainbow colors bright enough to be the middle of the day.

Bright enough, too, to see the lone human figure curled up in a fetal position on the ground—the figure of a red-headed child.

Without a word, Mom sprinted down the three steps from the porch and bolted across the yard. As fireworks shot randomly around her, she scooped up Boom and ran, heading for the corner of the house.

Amy fell in behind her, racing full-tilt through the fireworks barrage.

As they rounded the front of the house, finally out of the line of fire, sirens wailed in the distance, getting closer. Through the trees, Amy could see fire truck lights flashing in the sky, fast approaching.

Then, looking back, she saw flames leaping from the windows of the house, lashing angrily out of the empty sockets.

Still, the night echoed with booms and shrieks, pounding relentlessly from the backyard war zone.

*****

According to the paramedics, Boom was fine—just upset, as he should be. After all, the disaster was his fault.

Unable to wait another night to try the fireworks, he'd sneaked out to the shed when Mom and Amy were asleep, taking the key with him. He'd meant to set off a single bottle rocket, but he'd burned himself while lighting it and dropped the match in the shed. Another firework had blown instead and set off a chain reaction in the pile.

The rest was history.

"I'm sorry! I'm so sorry!" He bawled like a baby as the paramedics treated the burn on his hand. "I ruined everything!"

Mom didn't comfort him. She was too busy talking to police about all the illegal fireworks she'd been storing in her shed.

As for Amy, she stood and stared at the smoldering house, still stunned at what had happened. A firefighter had wrapped her in a blanket, and she held it tight around her, feeling like she was stuck in a bad dream.

"Oh my God." Grandpa walked up beside her, looking sadder than she'd ever seen him. "This is all my fault. My fault."

Amy said nothing. The fireworks had stopped long ago, but her ears still rang from the cacophony they'd caused.

"I just wanted this Fourth of July to be perfect for you kids," said Grandpa. "I wanted it to be perfect after what happened...but I just made things worse."

Firefighters stomped out of the house, pulling off their face masks. The fire was out, though it still wasn't clear to Amy how much damage had been done.

When Mom finally broke away from the cops and came over, Amy had a bad feeling about what she was going to say. Dread filled her like a cloud of smoke.

"So much for the fireworks spectacular," said Mom. "And so much for the house. I don't even know if the insurance will cover it."

"Oh God," said Grandpa.

"We'll be lucky if we don't get charged for stockpiling illegal fireworks," said Mom.

"I'll talk to the police," said Grandpa. "I'll tell them it was my fault, and..."

Mom chopped her hand through the air. "*No.* Please don't make this any *worse,* Dad."

"So what do we do?" asked Amy. "What's next?"

"As soon as they'll let me, I'm going to get in the house and see what I can salvage," said Mom. "You both can help with that, anyway."

"I don't think I can," said Amy. "I'm so tired, I can hardly stand up."

Just then, Kim approached from the street. "You can sleep at my house, if you'd like."

Amy looked expectantly at Mom. "Can I? Just for a few hours?"

"She'll need the rest before we go to Washington," said Kim.

Mom shook her head. "I'm sorry, but Washington's off the table."

Amy's feeling of dread blossomed into awful reality.

"What?"

"After what just happened?" Mom was adamant. "We don't even know where we're going to *live*."

"You can stay with me," said Grandpa.

"Your house is tiny," said Mom.

"I'll do what it takes," said Grandpa. "We'll make it work."

"That's *not* our only problem." Mom folded her arms over her chest. "It might not even be our *biggest* problem."

"Please let me go to D.C.," said Amy. "*Please*."

"No," Mom said firmly. "I need all of us here until I get this figured out."

"But it's just one day!" said Amy.

"Our *lives* have just been blown to *smithereens*," snapped Mom. "I need you *here*. End of story."

With that, she turned and marched off to the ambulance, where the paramedics had finished treating Boom.

"This is bad," said Kim. "This is really, really bad."

Amy just stood there and glared. Across the yard, she saw a female paramedic give Boom a lollipop as he hopped off the bumper of the ambulance, and her blood ran cold.

"It'll be okay, honey," said Grandpa. "Everything happens for a reason."

Amy didn't answer. She wasn't in the mood for platitudes, to say the least.

"I could ask my mom to talk to her," offered Kim. "Maybe she could convince her to let you go."

Amy thought for a moment, then shook her head. "Thanks anyway. That might just make things worse."

Kim reached out and touched her arm. "I'm so sorry,

Amy. I wish none of this had happened. I really do."

"Thanks. Me, too." When she said it, Amy was thinking not just of that night, but of everything leading up to it. She was thinking of Paul Newman coming to town and Dad and Mark leaving and all the sadness and confusion in between.

Once again, she remembered Michael Ontkean skating at the War Memorial. The striptease music played in her mind: *Da da da...da DA da da...da da da...da DA da da...*

And it was then that the tears finally started rolling down her cheeks, glistening in the flashing red lights of the fire trucks and police cars.

*****

"Here ya go, sweetheart." The burly, bald cook in the white t-shirt and smock stained with chili sauce banged a plate full of hot dogs on the counter in front of Amy. "Two with everything."

"Thanks." Amy slid the plate to the end of the counter, where Mom was paying for the food.

"Enjoy your picnic." The cook smirked and let out a little burp. "Happy Bicentennial."

So that was what it had come to. Instead of spending the Fourth of July in D.C. for the show of the century, she was stuck in Johnstown with Mom and Boom.

Whoop-de-doo.

"Here." Mom handed her a clear plastic cup full of water, then got an empty cup from the stack on the counter and filled it from a tap that was mounted there. It was a tradition at the Coney Island Lunch restaurant—a free glass of water with each purchase.

When she'd finished filling the cup, Mom headed for one of the orange tables along the wall, where Boom was already sitting. She put her tray on the table and lowered herself onto the bright green bench beside her son.

Amy sat across from them, staring at the hot dogs on her bright green plate. As much as she loved Coney Island's food, she wished she were anywhere but there at that moment—as far away as possible.

But that just wasn't in the cards for her.

"Eat up, guys." Mom handed Boom a hot dog—plain, on a bun, which was practically sacrilege in that place—and picked up one of her own. "I know it's not our usual cookout food, but it'll have to do."

There were so many things Amy wanted to say to her, to both of them, none of them good...but she held back the words. Instead, she grabbed one of the hot dogs on her plate and took a bite.

As usual, it was delicious—not that she was going to admit it. The mix of hot dog, chili, onions, mustard, and salt and pepper on a perfectly toasted bun was heavenly. It was the one bright spot in an otherwise lousy day.

It brought back good memories of Dad, too. He'd always loved Coney Island hot dogs, especially when he'd been drinking. He'd often brought her there for a late-night treat after he'd returned from making the rounds of his favorite bars. She'd loved spending time with him, even with his voice a little too loud and the alcohol strong on his breath.

"At least we salvaged some things at the house," Mom said between bites. "Some clothes and belongings. It wasn't a *total* loss."

Amy didn't answer. For one thing, she was in the worst mood ever over missing D.C. For another, she was utterly exhausted after spending the whole day digging for possessions in the rubble from the fire.

It was evening now, just after seven, and she was ready to collapse. Falling into a deep sleep and waking up the next morning seemed like the perfect way to put this god-awful day behind her.

There was just one small problem with that plan. She still didn't know where she was going to sleep that night.

"So where are we staying?" she asked.

"Grandpa's," said Mom. "But just for tonight."

"What about after that?" Boom actually sounded meek for a change. He hadn't been himself since he'd burned down the house.

"Well, I didn't want to say anything until it was definite," said Mom, "but I think we're going to stay with my friend Bonnie for a while."

Amy's shoulders slumped. Bonnie was nice, but her kids were rotten, and she lived in a neighborhood on the far side of Johnstown from Roxbury. It was nowhere near Kim, Roxbury Park, or anything else that Amy enjoyed.

"I have to call her tomorrow to find out for sure," said Mom. "But I can't imagine she'll say no."

Amy's next bite of the hot dog didn't taste as good as the last. The thought of moving in with Bonnie and her nasty kids made her heart sink...though she intended to keep it to herself, given the circumstances.

But Boom, for once, said exactly what she was thinking.

"I don't wanna stay with Bonnie."

Mom frowned. "But you always have fun when we visit her."

"No." Boom shook his head forcefully. "I don't wanna do it."

"It'll be fine." Mom looked at Amy for support. "Won't it, honey?"

But Amy didn't back her up. She just finished her first hot dog and washed it down with lukewarm water.

"I wish you never got that part in the movie," said Boom. "I wish Paul Newman never told Dad to leave."

"Well, he didn't," said Mom. "Dad just took what he said the wrong way."

"I was there!" snapped Boom. "I heard it! So did she!"

He pointed a finger at Amy.

And he was right. She thought back to that moment, just after the big parade, when she and Boom had run over to see Mom with Dad close behind. Mom had been standing by the white Lincoln Continental, chatting with Paul Newman in his hockey uniform.

And Dad, who'd been drunk, had pushed between them, face to face with Paul himself.

Dad had told Paul to leave his wife alone or he'd let him have it. Paul had told him to back off, there was nothing going on and never had been.

Then Dad had said that was the only reason she'd gotten a part in the movie, because she'd been running around with Paul behind Dad's back.

Again, Paul had denied the accusations. After that, Dad had taken a swing, but Paul had ducked and thrown him against the hood of the car. He'd gotten Dad in a hold, keeping his arm locked tight against his back.

Then he'd said it, loud enough for all of us to hear. He'd said the words that had broken up our family—even though he hadn't meant for that to happen.

"Do yourself a favor, buddy," he'd said. "Focus in on this great family you've got here and give the booze a rest."

Which, it turned out, had been the absolute wrong thing to say to Dad.

"Tell *me* to focus in?" he'd howled as a cop had dragged him away. "How about if I *focus in* on living my own *life* for a change!"

And he'd never looked back.

And Amy had never stopped looking back to that moment.

"Remember, Amy?" said Boom. "You remember what he told Dad, don't you?"

Amy pushed away her second hot dog. She wasn't hungry anymore.

"Yeah," she said. "And Mom's right."

Boom pounded the table with his fist. "No! That's not what you're supposed to—"

"Dad *did* take it the wrong way," said Amy, and then she got up and went to the counter for another cup of water.

"Hey, kid," said the burly counterman as she reached for a fresh cup. "What's a Fourth of July picnic without this?" He pulled out a cigarette lighter, flipped it open, and flicked the switch, raising a flame from the nozzle.

Then he laughed. "Just for you, kid! Enjoy the fireworks!"

*****

Blam!

Amy jumped as two bratty little boys set off a firecracker on the sidewalk outside Point Stadium. Though she was going to see the fireworks display at the Point—coerced by Mom, who wanted to show the flag for her bosses at Glosser Bros.—she was still a little rattled from her explosive experience of the night before.

She hesitated on the threshold, nearly turning and walking away...but Mom looked back and bobbed her head, summoning her inside. Though attending the Fourth of July production in downtown Johnstown was about the last thing Amy wanted to do, she rolled her eyes and followed.

She just had to get through this night, then deal with the rest of what was coming. It was just the way things were, given the circumstances.

"Well hello there!" Bill Glosser strode toward them, wearing a stars-and-stripes tie and a navy-blue pinstriped suit and carrying a thin sheaf of papers. As usual, plumes of smoke rolled out of his pipe, the stem clenched between his teeth as if attached there. "Good to see the Lindsey family won't let such a trivial thing as a house fire keep them from attending this soiree."

"Hello, Bill." Mom looked around at the stands, which were packed with people. "Looks like you've got a decent crowd tonight."

"Don't tell me that," said Bill. "You'll get me nervous before my big speech."

He chuckled, and so did Mom. Amy didn't react,

though, and Boom just looked like he wanted to run wild—though Mom kept his hand clamped in her own.

Just then, the organist started playing "God Bless America," and the audience applauded.

"That's my cue." Bill straightened his tie, adjusted his pipe, and turned, starting toward the podium set up on the pitcher's mound. But then he paused and looked back at Amy. "Sorry you missed out on that big honor I told you about the other day, sweetheart. When you said you weren't going to be here, we found someone else to kick things off."

"That's all right." Amy wasn't in the mood anyway. "I understand."

"Maybe for the Tricentennial, yeah?" Bill flapped the sheaf of papers, then resumed his course toward the podium.

"Let's go grab a seat," said Mom.

They ended up sitting in the front row, in a special section reserved for Glosser's employees. They were right by the concession stand, which of course caught Boom's attention as soon as his butt hit the bleacher.

As for Amy, the clock was already ticking in her head. Mom had promised they wouldn't stay long, and she was going to hold her to it.

At least that was the plan. But as Bill made his opening remarks, and local singers led the crowd in one patriotic song after another, Mom gave no sign of leaving.

Even when they trotted out the Cambria County Junior Miss finalists in all their teenage glory, Mom stayed in place. She didn't evacuate during the endless introduction of the Bicentennial committee members or the speech by Mayor

Herb Pfuhl, either.

The sky darkened, and the stadium lights flashed to life. Amy's impatience grew to the point where she actually jabbed Mom with an elbow—but Mom paid no attention. Were they *ever* going to get out of there?

Finally, Bill returned to the podium, and Mom jumped to her feet, clapping and cheering. So did the rest of the reserved section, and most of the crowd followed suit.

Bill's voice boomed from the P.A. system. "And now, ladies and gentlemen, the moment you've all been waiting for! The Bicentennial Fourth of July fireworks, sponsored by the Glosser Bros. and Gee Bee department stores!"

Everyone in the stadium applauded and cheered. This *was* what they'd all been waiting for.

"To start this spectacular event, we have a very special guest," said Bill. "She may have lost her home in a fire last night, but she's here tonight to launch the greatest fireworks display in Johnstown history!"

Amy's eyes widened. Had she heard him correctly?

The answer was yes, she had.

"Amy Lindsey, come on out here!" said Bill.

Amy was completely surprised. Everyone clapped and shouted her name...except Boom, who just slumped and gaped in dejected disbelief.

"Go ahead, honey." Mom grinned and pointed at the podium. "You heard the man."

Amy rose and started across the field—then stopped and turned. "Come on!" She gestured for Boom to join her.

And he didn't need convincing. Leaping to his feet, he charged out after her, grinning like a maniac.

"Stay with me." She gripped his arm tight. "Don't do *anything* till I tell you to."

"Okay okay okay!" Boom nodded excitedly.

And she led him to the podium where Bill was waiting.

"Good for you!" Bill said between puffs of pipe smoke. "You brought your little brother."

Amy and Boom just smiled.

"Right this way, then."

As Bill invited them to join him, Amy saw a wooden box with a big red button atop the podium. A thick bundle of wires ran out of it, snaking all the way across the field.

"All right, you two." Bill pulled his pipe out and gestured with the stem at the big red button. "We're all going to count down from ten. When we get to zero, hit that button. Got it?"

"Got it!" said Boom.

Amy just nodded.

"Here we go!" Bill waved his pipe in the air, and the stadium lights went out. Then he leaned over the podium and spoke into the mic again. "Count with me, folks!"

The crowd applauded.

"Ten!" said Bill. "Nine! Eight!"

Boom's hand shook as it hovered over the button. Amy held her hand just above, ready to grab him if he jumped the gun.

But he didn't. Not this time.

"Seven!" said Bill. "Six!"

The organist hit a dramatic chord each time Bill announced a number. The voices of everyone in the stadium joined together in a chorus of anticipation.

"Five!" said Bill. "Four! Three!"

The cords in Boom's hand flexed, and Amy thought he might hit the button early...but he didn't.

Her heart raced as the countdown neared its end.

"Two!" shouted Bill. "One!"

Amy and Boom's hands came down on the button at the same time.

For a moment, nothing happened...just long enough for Amy to wonder if something had gone wrong.

Then, she heard a loud hiss from behind her, in the direction of the Stonycreek River. She spun in time to see a smoky trail rise into the air.

And then it exploded in a burst of brilliant red.

Another one followed, hissing up and bursting into a sphere of cobalt blue...and another soared up after that and became a flare of bright white.

From that point on, the fireworks kept coming—shell after shell blazing to life above the stadium as a recording of "The Stars and Stripes Forever" blared over the P.A. Fireballs of every color blossomed in the night, casting the upturned faces of the spectators in mingled shades of green and gold and pink and red and blue.

When the biggest, most exciting blasts unfolded overhead, the crowd let out the usual oohs and ahhs. Little kids jumped to their feet and shrieked with delight, pointing and describing the dazzling lights.

Meanwhile, Boom and Amy watched it all hand in hand from the field. He beamed and laughed and jounced as if nothing bad had happened in the past 24 hours—as if their family's future was not uncertain in the extreme.

Amy forgot it all, too, and just lost herself in the show. Smiling, she gazed at the flares and flashes, listened to the booms and whistles without flinching. Not once did she think of Dad or *Slap Shot* or the burned-out house or going to live at Bonnie's.

She just melted into the play of lights and sound, enjoying the show though it surely didn't measure up to the extravaganza in D.C. Though it didn't come close to any of the shows she'd seen with Dad at her side, back when her family was still whole.

All that mattered for a while were the *whumps* and the *wheees,* the whites and the yellows and reds, the warm breeze and the heat of her little brother's hand clasped in hers.

*****

When the fireworks ended, and the stadium lights came up, Bill Glosser grinned at Amy and Boom. "So what do you two think? Did we put on a good show for our nation's 200th birthday?"

Amy and Boom both nodded.

"I agree." Bill puffed on his pipe. "The founding fathers would have been proud."

"It was *great!*" said Boom.

"Well, you two certainly did your part." Bill looked past them, then, and raised his voice. "Wouldn't you fellas agree?"

Amy turned and saw three men approach, all of them Glosser VIPs.

"One hundred percent." A balding, cheerful cousin of Bill's, Fred Glosser was in charge of construction for the Gee Bee stores. "We couldn't have done it without them."

Fred's brother, Izzy, was a tall, athletic guy who also

worked in the Gee Bee division. "You started that show like a couple of pros."

"I know talent when I see it," said bearded, dark-haired Paul, who ran the grocery division. "We'll have to keep them in mind, the next time we need a button pushed."

The four Glossers all laughed and patted Amy and Boom on the shoulders.

"Thanks again," said Bill, saluting with his smoldering pipe before turning away to chat with his family.

Amy realized it was time to go. "Come on, Boom. Let's go find Mom."

The rest of the crowd had the same idea, and they got separated in the rush for the gate. Amy got spun around once, then twice, and ended up falling when the kids who'd set off a firecracker earlier crashed past her.

Luckily, someone caught her from behind...and a pair of friendly faces leaned in to smile in front of her.

"Amy!" One was Ruby Shaffer from the soda fountain. She wore a red, white, and blue sweatshirt and a foam tiara like the Statue of Liberty's. "Just the girl we were looking for!"

"That's right." The other face, nearly identical, belonged to Ruby's twin sister, Ruth. She wore exactly the same outfit as Ruby. "We've been waiting for you since the show ended."

Amy was glad to see them but still unsteady on her feet and flustered. "Hi, guys."

"There's someone we want you to see," said Ruby.

"Someone *important*," said Ruth. "Are you ready to see him?"

"Well, I..." Amy frowned.

FOURTH OF JULY AT GLOSSER'S

Ruby leaned closer and whispered in her ear. "He's right behind you."

Puzzled, Amy looked back...and nearly fell again.

Her heart pounded, and she let out a cry of surprise and delight. Quickly regaining her footing, she whirled and threw her arms around the person who'd caught her—one of the last people she had expected to see on that night.

"I can't believe it!" Tears gushed from her eyes. "I can't believe you're here!"

"Of course I'm here," said her big brother, Mark, whom she hadn't seen in weeks. "You didn't think I'd miss out on the Point Stadium fireworks, did you?"

Ruth and Ruby waved and moved on with the crowd, but Amy was oblivious. Mark had her undivided attention.

"When did you...how did you...?" She didn't want to let go of him.

"I got in tonight, right before the fireworks," said Mark. "After what happened at the house, I had a feeling you'd be here."

"You know about the fire?"

"Boom called me," said Mark. "It sounded like you guys could use a hand."

"You drove all the way today?" asked Amy. "All the way from..." She stopped, because she didn't know where he and Dad had been living. They never called.

"All the way from Arlington." Mark nodded, stepped back, and pulled something from the front pocket of his jeans. "And I picked up a little something for you on my way out of D.C. today."

He laid a silver coin in her palm, a commemorative coin with the Bicentennial logo on one side and the

American flag on the other. It gleamed in the glow of the stadium lights, flashing as she moved it around.

"Oh, Mark." Amy thought she might break down and cry on the spot. Had Boom told him she couldn't go to see the fireworks in D.C. as she'd planned? Was that why he'd brought her a souvenir?

In the end, it didn't matter. All she cared about was that he was there—though his presence put a question in her mind, a question she had to ask.

"Is Dad here, too? Did he come with you?"

Mark shook his head. "I don't even know where he is, to tell you the truth. He talked about going to Hollywood to find Paul Newman, but who knows? He took off a couple weeks ago."

Amy slumped. As much as she hated her father for what he'd done, a part of her had still hoped he'd come back with Mark.

But maybe the one surprise guest would be enough.

"So anyway," said Mark. "What would you say if I stuck around a while and helped get the house fixed up?"

Amy just stared at him, stunned.

"I've been working, so I've got some money," Mark continued. "And I could get some buddies of mine to lend a hand."

Still, Amy was speechless.

"Do you think Mom would go along with that?" asked Mark. "We could camp out and rebuild, get the place livable again. Then none of you would have to go stay at Bonnie's."

"Oh, Mark." Tears flowed from Amy's eyes.

"I mean, unless you *want* to live with those bratty kids

of hers," said Mark, "way out there in Tanneryville."

Amy shook her head. "She'll go along with it," she said. "She *has* to."

"Well, good." Mark smiled and reeled her in for a hug. "We'll stick together and make this work."

It was then that Amy remembered what Paul Newman had said to her, the one thing he'd told her and her alone. She'd been so angry with him for so long, she'd kept herself from thinking about it—but now it came back to her.

She'd gone to Johnnie's Restaurant on Main Street for breakfast with Mom, Mark, and Boom, and Paul had been eating at the bar, about to leave town. Mom had thanked him for everything and said goodbye, and Paul had hugged her...and then, as she and Boom had headed for a table, Paul had caught Amy in a handshake and said one last thing.

"Take care of what you've got there, kid," he'd told her, nodding in the direction of Mom, Mark, and Boom. "They'll do the same for you."

The words echoed in her head as Mark held her tight, his embrace a promise that things would get better.

"Don't worry," he said. "I'll get you through this, I swear."

"Thanks," said Amy, smiling through her tears. "I swear I'll get *you* through this, too."

ABOUT THE AUTHOR

USA Today-bestselling author and editor Robert Jeschonek grew up in Johnstown, Pennsylvania and spent many happy hours as a kid in the Glosser Bros. Department Store. Since then, he has gone on to write lots of books and stories, including *Long Live Glosser's, Penn Traffic Forever, Christmas at Glosser's, Easter at Glosser's, Halloweeen at Glosser's, Thanksgiving at Glosser's, A Glosser's Christmas Love Story, Valentine's Day at Glosser's, Fear of Rain, Richland Mall Rules,* and *Death By Polka* (which are all set in and around Johnstown). He has written a lot of other cool stuff, too, including *Star Trek* and *Doctor Who* fiction and *Batman* comics. His young adult fantasy novel, *My Favorite Band Does Not Exist*, won a Forward National Literature Award and was named a top ten first novel for youth by *Booklist* magazine. His work has been published around the world in over a hundred books, e-books, and audio books. You can find out more about them at his website, www.robertjeschonek.com, or by looking up his name on Facebook, Twitter, or Google. As you'll see, he's kind of crazy...in a *good* way.

ACKNOWLEDGEMENTS

Special thanks to Esther Vorhauer and Laryssa Duncan of the Cambria County Library Reference Department for their research assistance in support of this book (and others). Their diligence, expertise, and generosity make it possible for writers like me to bring the past to life in memorable ways.

To support their efforts and the Cambria County Library system, click the Donate Now button at the library's website: www.cclsys.org.

ANOTHER GREAT JOHNSTOWN STORY NOW AVAILABLE FROM ROBERT JESCHONEK

ALSO AVAILABLE FROM PIE PRESS:

A GLOSSER'S CHRISTMAS LOVE STORY

BY ROBERT JESCHONEK

With her fiancé far away fighting a war in Korea, Sarah faces a blue Christmas in Johnstown, Pennsylvania in 1953. But going to work as an elf at Glosser's Department Store turns her holiday upside-down. Santa Claus, played by fellow employee Frank, falls beard over sleighbells for her. When the magic of the season at Glosser's lights a spark of romance between them, Sarah is torn between the man at war and the one in the St. Nick outfit. On the night before Christmas, she must make a fateful choice that changes everything...and leads her to a crossroads 63 years later at the famous musical Christmas tree in Johnstown's Central Park.

AND NOW, A SPECIAL PREVIEW OF A GLOSSER'S CHRISTMAS LOVE STORY...

A GLOSSER'S CHRISTMAS LOVE STORY

Johnstown, 1953

"You dropped something." The young man with the bright green eyes and red hair held up a 20-lb. frozen turkey and grinned. "Here you go."

Sarah Jensen stopped in the frozen food aisle of the Glosser Bros. grocery store and shook her head. "Not *my* turkey, thanks."

"But it is!" The guy pushed the frozen turkey toward her. "I clearly saw it fall out of the pocket of your sweater."

Sarah shrugged and sighed. She wasn't in the mood to goof around that morning, not after the letter she'd gotten before coming to work. "You must be confusing me with someone else."

"Not a chance." The guy's smile turned charming. "There's *no way* I could ever confuse you with anyone else."

The smile made Sarah hesitate. She was 23 years old,

after all, and he was...he was...

Not completely unattractive. His eyes were bright as emeralds, his hair red as firelight. He was six feet tall, with a slim, athletic build and muscular shoulders. And he was about her age or a little younger, perhaps a little older.

But no. She had her reasons for not socializing these days. And besides... "I need to get back to my register," she told him. "My lunch break is over."

"So?" He lowered the turkey, revealing the Glosser Bros. nametag pinned to the chest of his white button-down shirt. "I'm not even *on* break."

The tag, stamped with the name "Frank," caught Sarah off guard. She hadn't known he was a fellow employee. She'd never even seen him before he shoved the turkey in her face.

Not that it made any difference. "Look, I really have to get back to my register," she said.

"Then what am I supposed to do with *this?*" He turned the turkey over in his hands, looking forlorn.

It was then she was seized by the inexplicable impulse to throw him a bone. "Put it in the oven for six and a half hours at 325," she said. "Either that, or roll it down the aisle and use it to bowl for customers."

"Brilliant!" Frank perked up. "You're a genius..." He peered at the nametag pinned to Sarah's gray sweater. "...you *Sarah*, you."

"That's what they tell me." Sarah smirked. "I'm a genius, all right."

As she started to walk away, Frank stepped in front of her. "See you around?" He smiled expectantly.

"I guess so." Reaching up, she pushed a lock of her chestnut brown hair behind her right ear. "Though I've never seen you around before today."

"That's because this is my first day on the job." He winked. "But you'll be seeing me a lot more from now on."

"Is that so?" Sarah looked toward the checkouts in the front of the store. If she didn't get back to her post soon, someone would come looking for her.

"Absolutely." Frank nodded enthusiastically. "I'm like a bad penny. I keep turning up."

Sarah shrugged and headed for the checkouts. Frank backed away and disappeared in the frozen food department.

Up front, she returned to her register, apologizing for being late to the girl who'd been covering for her. The girl, a chatty redhead, didn't seem to care as she stepped away from the checkout and Sarah replaced her.

As the next customer put her items on the counter, Sarah punched their prices into the register. She slid cans of corn and green beans into the bagging area at the end of the counter, and someone caught them.

At first, Sarah didn't look to see who was doing the bagging. But as she finished ringing everything up, she turned...and there he was.

Frank Halloran himself grinned back at her as he loaded the items into big brown paper bags.

Sarah just stared. She hadn't expected to see him there.

"Ma'am?" Frank was talking to the customer. "Shall I carry these upstairs for you?" Offering to haul purchases was expected, since the grocery store was located in the basement of Glosser's department store. It was a long walk up and out to the parking lot or on-street parking, especially with a heavy load of groceries.

"Yes, please." The customer, a heavyset middle-aged

woman in a pale green coat and squat cream hat, nodded. "My car is out back in the lot." With that, she paid Sarah, got her receipt, and briskly started toward the nearby flight of stairs to the first floor.

Frank followed with a bag in each arm. He winked at Sarah as he followed the customer, mouthing four words that made her smile in spite of herself.

Penny for your thoughts?

*****

What happens next? Find out in A GLOSSER'S CHRISTMAS LOVE STORY, on sale now!

If you liked this book, you'll *love* these!

LONG LIVE GLOSSER'S

CHRISTMAS AT GLOSSER'S

EASTER AT GLOSSER'S

HALLOWEEN AT GLOSSER'S

THANKSGIVING AT GLOSSER'S

VALENTINE'S DAY AT GLOSSER'S

PENN TRAFFIC FOREVER
(A History of the Penn Traffic Department Store)

RICHLAND MALL RULES
(A History of the Richland Mall in Johnstown)

THE GLORY OF GABLE'S
(A History of Altoona's Gable's Department Store)

FEAR OF RAIN
(A Johnstown Flood Story)

THE MASKED FAMILY
(A Cambria County Story)

NOW ON SALE EVERYWHERE ONLINE
OR BY REQUEST AT YOUR LOCAL BOOKSTORE
Ask your bookseller to search by title at Amazon,
Ingram, or Baker and Taylor.

Made in the USA
Middletown, DE
17 June 2023